FOR MY DAD, WHO HAS GIVEN ME THE TOOLS
TO TAKE ON ANY CHALLENGE, AND RICKY, NATHAN, AND ALEX,
WHO I LOVE BUILDING A LIFE WITH—I LOVE YOU MORE. –J.L.B.D.

FOR GRANDPA ED AND GRANDPA RAFA. -L.R.

A NOTE FROM THE AUTHOR:

In 2015, my husband, Ricky, was diagnosed with a brain tumor. Despite everything he's faced, he continues to inspire our family and many others with his courage and strength. In honor of him, as well as the brain tumor patients and childhood cancer patients we've met on this journey, a gray ribbon and a gold ribbon have been included in the illustrations to raise awareness and show support for all those affected by these diagnoses.

STERLING CHILDREN'S BOOKS
New York

An Imprint of Sterling Publishing Co., Inc.
122 Fifth Avenue
New York, NY 10011

ISBN 978-1-4549-3232-1

Distributed in Canada by Sterling Publishing Co., Inc.
c/o Canadian Manda Group, 664 Annette Street
Toronto, Ontario M6S 2C8, Canada
Distributed in the United Kingdom by GMC Distribution Services
Castle Place, 166 High Street, Lewes, East Sussex BN7 1XU, England
Distributed in Australia by NewSouth Books,
University of New South Wales. Sydney, NSW 2052, Australia

For information about custom editions, special sales, and premium and corporate purchases, please contact Sterling Special Sales at 800-805-5489 or specialsales@sterlingpublishing.com.

Manufactured in China

Lot #:
2 4 6 8 10 9 7 5 3
10/20

sterlingpublishing.com

When Grandpa Gives You A Toolbox

WRITTEN BY
JAMIE L. B. DEENIHAN

ILLUSTRATED BY
LORRAINE ROCHA

STERLING CHILDREN'S BOOKS
New York

You wanted a special house for your dolls.

But, surprise! It's a . . .

. . . TOOLBOX.

What should you do when Grandpa
gives you a toolbox for your birthday?

First, be patient. Grandpa will want to show you every single tool.

Next, compliment Grandpa as he shares photos of all the projects he's built since he was a kid.

Once Grandpa runs out of stories,
give him a hug, say thanks, and tell him you're off to
find a special place to keep your toolbox.

launch it into outer space,

feed it to a T.rex,

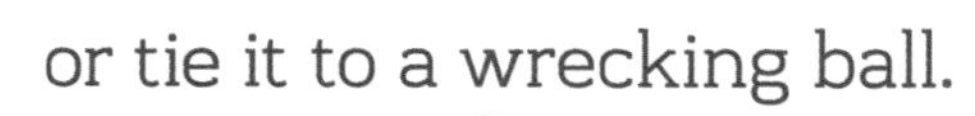

or tie it to a wrecking ball.

There are plenty of hiding spots right in your own backyard.

It'll be easy to forget about Grandpa's toolbox.

Until you meet someone in need and have an idea.

Maybe Grandpa's toolbox will be useful
just this one time.

As a new builder, you'll want to find an experienced project manager to help you get started.

Together, you'll create a plan and gear up.

SAFETY FIRST!

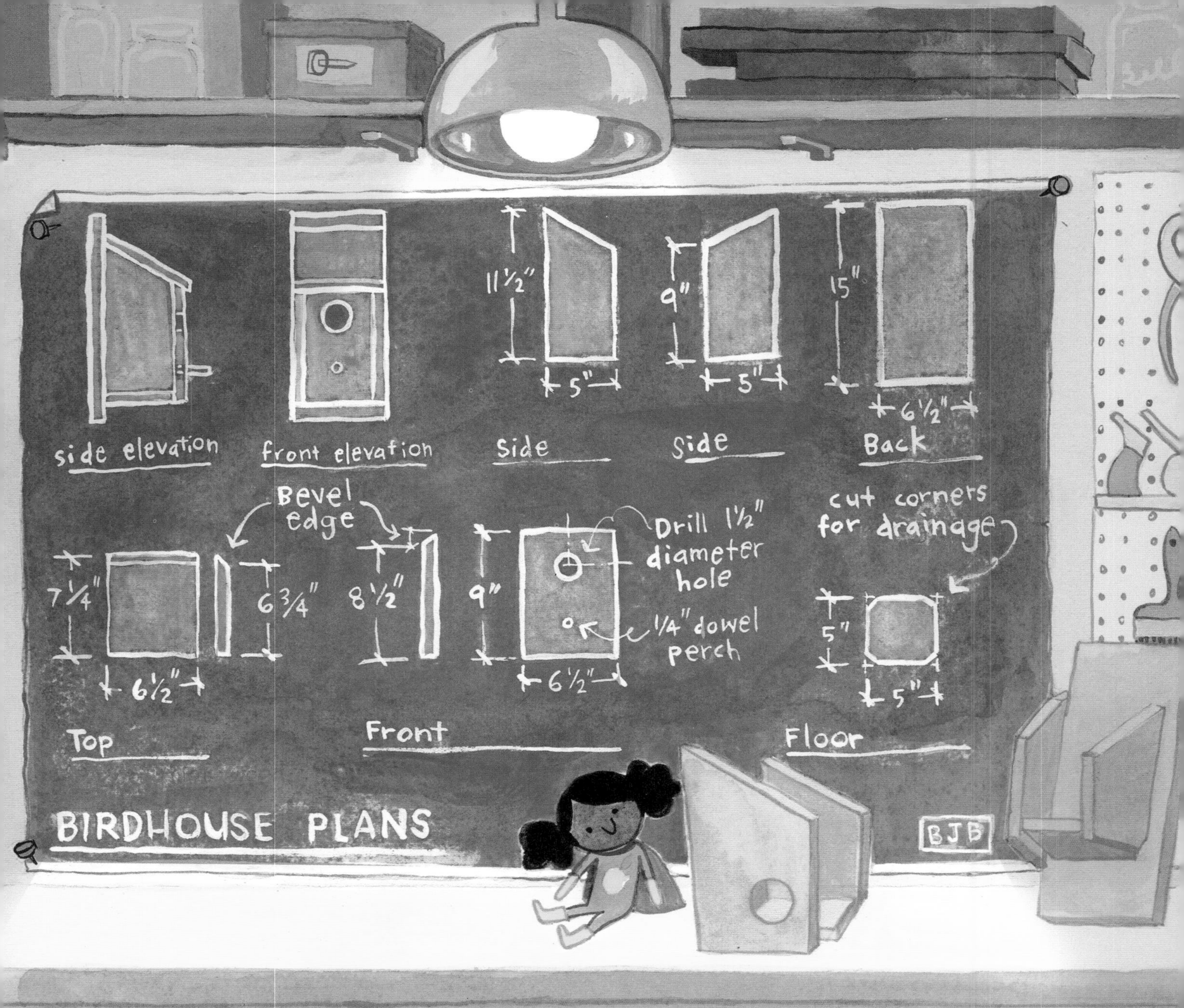

With guidance and lots of practice, you'll discover that you're actually quite handy.

BJB
paint

Your neighbor won't
complain about the noise,
though she will ask for
help with repairs . . .

. . . and recommend you to all her friends.

BJB

At the end of the day, they'll offer to pay you,
but you'll have an even better idea.

You and Grandpa will work together measuring and sawing,

drilling and hammering,

gluing and painting,

until finally, you've built exactly what you wanted.

A SPECIAL HOUSE
FOR YOUR DOLLS,

coffee
ABD
BJB

swing
slide
Treehouse Plans
By:
ABD
Fort

AND PLANS FOR YOUR NEXT PROJECT, TOO.

MEYER